Clifford's
Christmas

Norman Bridwell

SCHOLASTIC INC.

New York   Toronto   London   Auckland

Sydney   Mexico City   New Delhi   Hong Kong

For Jesse

ISBN 978-0-545-21596-1

Copyright © 1984 by Norman Bridwell.

All rights reserved. Published by Scholastic Inc.
SCHOLASTIC, CARTWHEEL BOOKS, and associated logos are trademarks and/or registered trademarks of Scholastic Inc.
CLIFFORD, CLIFFORD THE BIG RED DOG, BE BIG, and associated logos are trademarks and/or registered trademarks of Norman Bridwell.

Library of Congress Cataloging-in-Publication Data is available.

12 11 10 9   18 19 20

Printed in the U.S.A.   40
This edition first printing, September 2011

Hi! I'm Emily Elizabeth.
This is my dog, Clifford.
Guess what holiday it is!

We start celebrating Christmas on Thanksgiving.
Last year we went to the Thanksgiving Day parade.
Clifford loved the big balloons.

At the end of the parade, Santa Claus came to town.
The Christmas season had begun!

Soon it started to snow.

My friends and I made a snowman.
Clifford made one too.

Later we went to the pond to play ice hockey.
We were having a great time until . . .

We decided that Clifford shouldn't play
ice hockey anymore.

Christmas was getting closer and closer.
We counted the days.

One day Clifford saw some men digging up a tree.
He thought it would be a nice Christmas tree for us.

The tree was too big for our house . . .

but it was just right for Clifford's.

When Clifford was taking a nap,
my friends and I sneaked up on him
with some mistletoe.

Surprise!

At last it was Christmas Eve.

Clifford and I hung up his stocking.

I put some presents under Clifford's tree.

That night when we were sleeping
Santa came.

He landed on Clifford's roof.
He walked around looking
for a chimney . . .

Oops!

Clifford woke up.
He heard someone calling for help.

Clifford helped. What a surprise!

Oh no—the bag of toys!
It had fallen into Clifford's water bowl.
The toys were ruined.

Clifford felt terrible. He had to do something.
So he offered Santa his own Christmas presents
to give to the children.

Santa smiled and patted Clifford.

He told him not to worry.

Then with a wave of his magic mittens,

Santa made the toys new again.

After leaving some toys at my house,
Santa got back in his sleigh.
He said good-bye to Clifford, and away
he flew until next year.

On Christmas morning
Clifford and I opened our presents.
It was a wonderful day.

And Clifford is a wonderful dog.
He makes every day Christmas Day.